GERALD M^c BOING BOING

based on the Academy Award®–winning motion picture by

Dr. Seuss

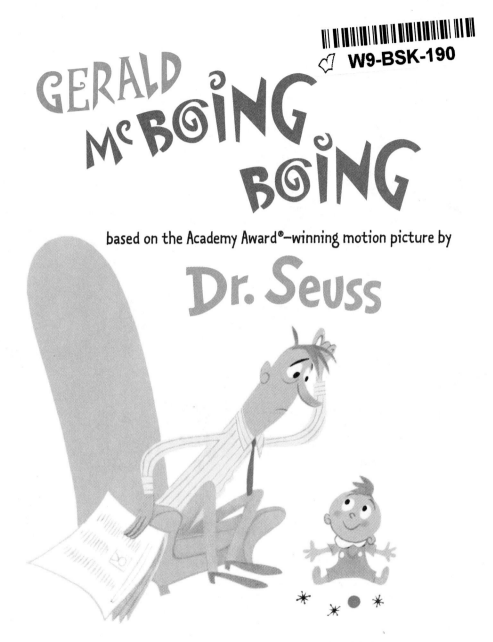

pictures adapted by MEL CRAWFORD

A GOLDEN BOOK • NEW YORK

Based on the movie *Gerald McBoing Boing,* copyright © 1950, renewed 1978 by Columbia Pictures Industries, Inc. All rights reserved under International and Pan-American Copyright Conventions. Published in the United States by Golden Books, an imprint of Random House Children's Books, a division of Random House, Inc., New York, and simultaneously in Canada by Random House of Canada Limited, Toronto. Originally published in 1952 in slightly different form by Simon and Schuster, Inc., and Artists and Writers Guild, Inc., and in 2000 in slightly different form by Random House, Inc. Golden Books, A Golden Book, A Little Golden Book, the G colophon, and the distinctive gold spine are registered trademarks of Random House, Inc.
Library of Congress Control Number: 2003103625
ISBN: 978-0-375-82721-1
www.seussentennial.com
www.goldenbooks.com
Printed in the United States of America
10 9 8 7 6 5 4

This is the story of Gerald McCloy
And the strange thing that happened
to that little boy.

They say it all started
    when Gerald was two—
That's the age kids start talking—
    least, most of them do.
Well, when he started talking,
    you know what he said?

He didn't talk words—
    he went BOING BOING! instead!
"What's that?" cried his father,
    his face turning gray,
"That's a very odd thing
    for a young boy to say!"

And poor Gerald's father
   rushed to the phone
And quick dialed the number
   of Doctor Malone.
"Come over fast!"
   the poor father pled.
"Our boy can't speak words—
   he goes BOING BOING instead!"

"I see," said the doctor,
   "it's just as you said.
He doesn't speak words—
   he goes BOING BOING instead!

"I've no cure for this.
I can't handle the case."
And he packed up his pills
and walked out of the place.

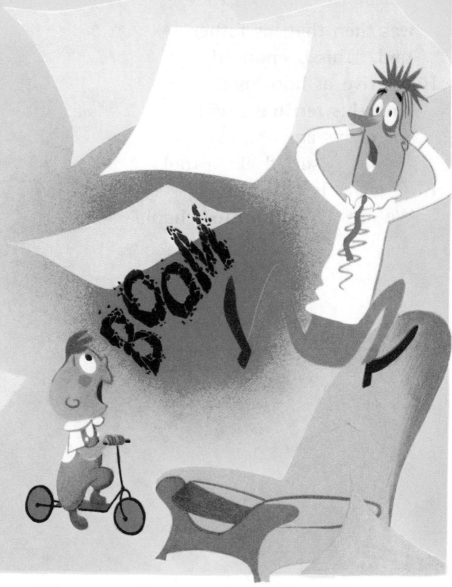

Then months passed, and Gerald
    got louder and louder
Till one day he went *BOOM!*
    like a big keg of powder!

It was then that his father
     said, "This is enough!
He'll drive us both mad
     with this terrible stuff!
A boy of his age
     shouldn't sound like a fool.
He's got to learn words.
     We must send him to school."

So Gerald marched off,
an obedient creature,

But he soon was back home
with a note from the teacher.
"From Public School Seven
to Mrs. McCloy:

Your little son Gerald's
a most hopeless boy.
We cannot accept him,
for we have a rule
That pupils must not go
Cuckoo in our school.
Your boy will go HONK
all his life, I'm afraid.
Sincerely yours, Fanny Schultz,
Teacher, First Grade."

And as little Gerald
grew older, he found
When a fellow goes **BAM!**
no one wants him around.

When a fellow goes *SKREEK!*
    he won't have any friends.
For once he says, "CLANG CLANG CLANG!"
    all the fun ends.

CLANG
CLANG

"Nyah nyah!" they all shouted,
"Your name's not McCloy!
You're Gerald McBoing Boing,
the noise-making boy!"

Poor Gerald decided
   that he had no place
At home, in the school—
   in the whole human race!

And so he concluded
that, drear and forlorn,
He would just disappear
in the thick of a storm.

But as he was boarding
a slow-moving freight,
A voice from the darkness
called out, "Stop, boy! Wait!"

"Aren't you Gerald McBoing Boing,
   the lad who makes squeaks?
My boy, I have searched
   for you many long weeks!
I can make you the most
   famous lad in the nation,
For I own the **BONG-BONG-BONG**
   Radio Station!

"I need a smart fellow
to make all the sounds,
Who can bark like a dog,
and bay like the hounds!

"Your GONG is terrific,
    your toot is inspired!
Quick come to BONG-BONG-BONG,
    McBoing Boing–you're hired!"

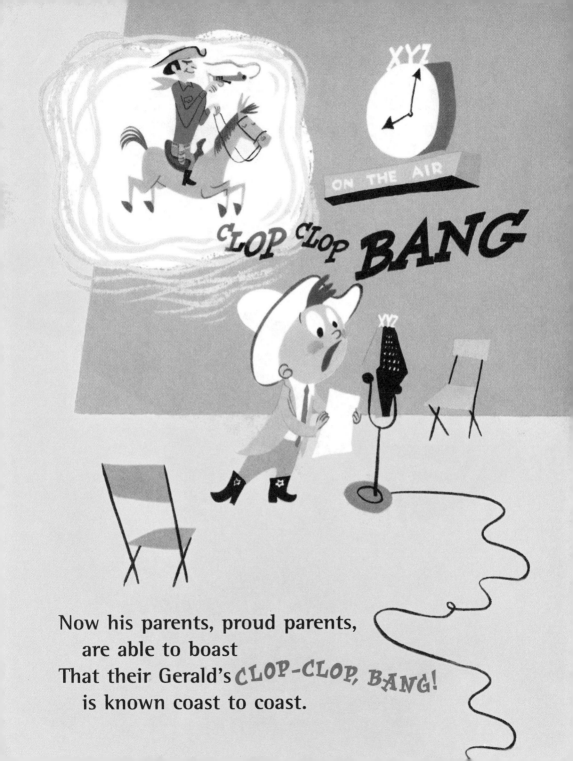

Now his parents, proud parents,
    are able to boast
That their Gerald's CLOP-CLOP, BANG!
    is known coast to coast.

Now Gerald is rich,
   he has friends, he's well fed,
'Cause he doesn't speak words,
   he goes BOING BOING instead!